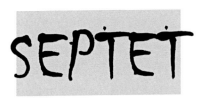

SEPTET

by Myrtle M. Burton

*To my one and
only Michèle
with love from
Mom*

RoseDog 🐾 Books

PITTSBURGH, PENNSYLVANIA 15222

To my daughter, Michele Agnes McLean, whose riches, as yet unrealized, are in her character.

INTRODUCTION

It is my opinion that reading is a blessing in many forms. Although all writings do not necessarily cheer us up, they have far-reaching results. Important stories about war and peace and individual movers and shakers nurture us mentally, and, by reading these stories, we benefit from them, adding their knowledge to what we already know. Even science fiction and horror stories feed our minds and exercise our emotions.

It is only nonfiction that we can debate. Fiction is opinion wrapped up in imagination. There is no true or false in a writer's opinion or imagination.

My stories are very short. The few minutes needed to read each of them can be fun, and readers may even be moved by certain passages. Only one story about my father is nonfiction. I introduced imaginary new people to myself in the other six.

ACKNOWLEDGMENTS

My gratitude lies with all my family members, still with me and deceased, who shaped my life through the years, and to all my friends who have given me reasons for expression, hope and stability.

Genuine appreciation has been earned by the publishers of my work, RoseDog Books, for unrestrained encouragement and professional guidance.

CONTENTS

ONE:
STELLA'S JUDGMENT

The hooded fan above Stella's stove was too low, too noisy, and too hard to clean. The neon bulb was dull. And, yes, the old sink was showing more rust near the faucets. Stella put the last few dishes on the drainboard, rinsed them down, and let out the dishwater. She stood quietly in thought. The picture in her mind made her smile. How about it? Suppose she wired the apartment with dynamite to detonate in half an hour: she could pick up Sambuca, her black cat, put him in his carrier, get out of harm's way outside with him, and then wait for the entire apartment to blow up. For Stella, an antidote to a blue mood, often, was simply having a sense of humor.

Instead of nuking the apartment, Stella turned off the harsh light and walked over to the couch where she sat with the TV remote, curled her feet under her, and turned on the television set. She clicked from one strident advertisement to another. Even the television fare was awful. She pushed the mute button and closed her eyes. The only sound was the clanking of the radiator as it huffed and puffed to heat up the place. Sambuca moved to her side and rolled over, looking up at Stella, and waiting for her to scratch his chin.

Jamie and Stella daCosta had rented a studio apartment near Amsterdam Avenue, on the west side of New York, when Jamie took a job in the city. From the street, the apartment building still displayed an attractive Art Deco design. The roof was elegantly rounded, and there was a modified Greek key tracing in the frieze. Most of the deterioration was on the inside. The countless tenants that had come and gone from the apartments left much to be done at costs that were simply out of any consideration whatsoever by this time. Jamie and Stella were struggling to get a bit of equity to manage the purchase of a co-op, and the shabby bathroom fixtures and out-of-date kitchen had to suit them for a while. They loved the city, but were often discouraged by the wealth they saw, wondering how they could ever enjoy even a fraction of the successes. Stella would sometimes feel encouraged when others would say, "Oh, my dears, you are still so very young!"

Leaving their families and friends in Westchester made hardly a ripple in their mutual closeness, and trains proved to be no big deal at all. They had given up their car; it was not a necessity in the city. Stella got a job at a Duane Reade drugstore around the corner, and she took courses at Hunter College some evenings, hoping to get involved in special education. She didn't want to pay anything on taxis or even subways if she could help it. Jamie had graduated early from the State University of New York at Purchase, upstate, eager to make his way in an accounting firm where he was now; it was his very first full-time white-collar job. The museums and entertainment for the masses were the best to be had at little cost, and they loved Central Park, the gift to people of all incomes. So, whatever their problems were, a great many things were pleasures for them, and, yes, they were "so very young." They were both twenty-two years old. At the moment, it wasn't depression in Stella for what they did not have; it was simply that she missed Jamie miserably when he had to go away for any time at all.

She wasn't asleep, but when the telephone shrieked, she jerked upward and Sambuca darted away. Even when she was expecting a call, the telephone was often jarring. She picked it up, ready for the telemarketing call to which she always tried to be polite, saying, "I'm sorry, I'm not interested," but this call was different. There was a vague recognition in Stella's mind. Of what, she did not know. The voice was a little muffled, perhaps deflected by something, and it was fast and direct. A woman's voice said, "Your husband is cheating on you. He's at José's on 43rd Street with Mildred Leverich right now." The caller then hung up.

Stella's state of mind had been low to begin with, but this was a blow. Her heart began to pound. She stood up to get her bearings, and then hurried to the door to make sure it was locked, feeling psychologically vulnerable, the voice sounding in her ears. Who had it been? How could this be true? Jamie was not expected until tomorrow night, and, at the moment, should still be in Washington. Images flashed through her head. Could he? Was she naïve herself? Was the caller someone she knew? Was it a crank? Should she call Jamie? (And say what? "Are you where you should be?"). Her mind darted from one possibility to another, trying to get an explanation. It all boiled down to whether or not she believed the caller. Mildred Leverich was a name that rang a bell, but she couldn't remember why she knew the name. Stella concentrated then on the sound of the voice, thinking of every aspect of the inflections and the words.

Stella adored her husband. Jamie daCosta had been her "dream come true." They had been married for only eighteen months, and her love for him always seemed to be getting stronger. She considered herself very fortunate; she had an easy-going outlook on life, was appreciative of the little things, and accepted everyone she met with an unquestioned right for anybody to be his or her own individual. She felt that modes of dress and quirks of character had every right to be part of a certain individual. She found reasons to accept even difficult people without malice. It was a mature outlook on life for a woman so young. Her friends, and Jamie's friends, loved her for that maturity and ready-generosity of spirit. She had reacted to the telephone call with confusion; she simply had not experienced so shocking a personal encounter before.

Jamie was handsome, of course, with wide dark eyes and thick, unruly dark hair, but he seemed unaware of his good looks when Stella saw women sizing him up. Stella was a charmer, too, petite and trim. She put aside some very fine men to date Jamie. However, she always felt she could be more attractive as his mate. She had her hair streaked, and she kept fit on her cycle machine, yet she wondered what more she could do to make herself more sophisticated.

At eleven o'clock, bewildered and frightened, Stella decided to call Jamie. He usually watched or listened to the late evening news and went to bed shortly afterward. She could just say she missed him like crazy and couldn't wait to get him back home tomorrow night.

At the hotel in Washington, a desk clerk told Stella that Mr. James daCosta had checked out that morning.

The next morning, Stella got ready for work like a robot. She had tossed most of the night, drifting into sleep only to have wild dreams in which she was crying, and he looked sad. Jamie's arrival time that evening could not come fast enough. The shuttle was scheduled to arrive around six, so he'd be home about seven, if all went as planned. She had decided not to say anything about the telephone call, but to wait and see how he would act.

He buzzed the intercom at 7:15 . Stella was tense when he came in, but his smile and his haste to embrace her were those of the usual loving Jamie, and she fell into his spell as she always did, telling herself that everything was normal, that the terrible call was a fluke. They had margaritas, which they both loved, and he chattered about his trip, holding her hands tight as he explained that he now knew what their home office looked like in Washington. He told her about the work they accomplished and the lovely wide streets of the Capital. He didn't mention leaving early.

Three days later, when Stella was checking in with the superintendent of the building, he handed her a pale green envelope. It had been dropped off, he said, half an hour ago by a man he hadn't seen before. Alone on the elevator, Stella tore the envelope open. The note inside was in block letters, and it said, "GET YOUR ACT TOGETHER, GIRL. HE TOOK THE AFTERNOON OFF." Stella began to shake. He had told her he'd be a little late because he had to see somebody about a new policy that the company was planning to offer to seniors. Stella gaped at the words on the paper, trying to make sense of them. She wondered about fingerprints. Was this something she should follow up on? She put it in a bureau drawer with some T-shirts and covered it up. On the verge of tears, she tried to come to grips with the unknown, but she really did not know what to do.

She had prepared chili the night before, so she placed it on a slow burner and put on an Edith Piaf CD. She sat quietly, waiting for Jamie, tormented and frightened. He hadn't arrived at seven, and she was beside herself. Almost in panic, she realized that she had to do something to occupy her mind. She decided to call a lady on the fourth floor whom she had befriended when they both happened to move in at the same time. They often chatted in the lobby. She didn't enjoy talking with Jan particularly because she had a negative view of most things, especially men, but Jan lived alone and had often invited Stella in for a drink. Stella had refused because she was always expecting Jamie to come home for dinner. Now, she was trying to make light of her nervous predicament and pass the time pretending to act normal.

"Hi, Jan. It's Stella from 306. I finally have a moment when I can sit back and relax. Can you come and have a drink with me? Jamie's working late tonight."

"Well, I don't believe it," Jan responded. She was so surprised that she stammered a little. "I...well, oh my goodness, the princess on the third floor is coming out of her shell. I'd love to come. Got some wine, or shall I bring some?"

Stella was surprised at the strange remarks from Jan, but she kept her composure and responded normally. "I have wine, red and white. See you in a bit?"

As Stella scurried to her semibare cupboard to find wine glasses, the telephone rang. It was Jamie telling her he'd be a little later than expected. Stella's stomach turned over, but she managed to keep calm. "I've invited Jan Davis in for a drink," she said. "I was feeling a bit lonely."

"That's great, Hon'. Maybe I'll see her when I get back. Won't be long."

Jan arrived with some fancy petit fours and a bottle of Merlot. "Hi, love. These are leftovers of a friend's leftovers. Didn't want to throw them out. You said you had wine, but I kinda favor this type, and one little bottle doesn't go very far. I'm so glad you called. How ya doin'?" Actually, Stella welcomed the irrepressible Jan at the moment. They settled in, facing each other on the only sofa in the apartment.

Jan babbled on. "What's goin'on, kiddo? You must admit that this is a surprise for me. I've hinted often enough, but you didn't bite."

"Oh, Jan, I'm sorry. I really am. I don't really know what to say. I guess I'm just used to a routine. I don't seem to know what else to do. I'm happy you're here. Cheers!" They raised their glasses.

"You know what the gossip is, Stella honey? Everybody thinks you don't want to share that handsome hunk of yours." She saw a serious look on Stella's face and backed down. "Oh, Stella, I'm sorry," she laughed. "Don't take it so seriously. C'mon, tell me about you, and let's have some fun. When do you expect Jamie home?"

"About now, I guess," Stella responded, "but he called. He's been delayed again."

"I'll run when he gets home. I'm helping Donna Schechter with the flyer for our co-op Halloween blast on the thirty-first. I'm supposed to call her. You and Jamie coming?"

"Oh, yes. I'm looking forward to it. It's a fact that we don't get out much. We're always trying to save money, but we love staying home, too, with Sambuca." They both laughed when the cat, ensconced under the table at their feet, looked up at the sound of his name.

"You're not alone there, honey. It ain't cheap in this town. By the way, how well do you know Donna?"

"Not well at all, actually. I've said 'hello' many times and we've passed the time o'day."

"Interesting. She said she knows you quite well."

"What?"

"That's what she said. She was mooning over your husband one night, and she was a little high when she said she'd sure like to have his shoes under her bed some night."

"I think that's disgusting."

"I think it's funny. Fat chance. But she tells me that she's broken up two marriages. You know how men are. She seems to find a way, but she's not all that great, do you think?"

"I never gave it a thought," Stella said.

"Just the same, keep an eye on that guy," Jan said, smiling.

The conversation was helping Stella put her thoughts together. She found herself animatedly saying to Jan, "Let me help with the brochures, Jan. I really need more to do. Are you doing them on the computer? Will you be going to Donna's soon? I'd like to get to know her better."

"Don't you…you know, don't you tell her what I said!" Jan said with real concern.

"I won't, my dear, not a word. I just want to get more involved. I'm not worried about my husband."

"Okay, we can get the folding done, and the sorting out and addressing. We're not going to use stamps. We'll just pass them into the in-house mail. Sure, you can help. I'll tell Donna when I call her."

The two women began to enjoy each other, and the wine helped quite a bit. Stella began to feel that a great burden had been lifted from her shoulders. Somehow, she really, really knew why. Maybe the faint trace of familiarity in that unexpected telephone call had given her a clue. She would have to figure out just where her beloved husband had been on two occasions, but that wouldn't be a problem.

Jamie came home at 9:30. Jan had gotten up to leave when he buzzed. They greeted each other cheerfully, and Stella was proud of him as he helped Jan with the door. He beamed when he hurried to Stella. He had been on Broad Street, downtown, and was noticeably tired from a long day. "I wanted you to be there, honey," he said, stroking her hair. "We went to Fraunces Tavern, and I just have to take you there soon. I want you to see the old building. It's wonderful! And the history! That's where George Washington said good-bye to his men at the end of the American Revolution. It was 1780 something. It's on Pearl Street. You'll love it. They have antiques on the upper floors that were used by Washington and his men, and I want you to see them." Yes, Jamie was tired, but lovingly expressive. "By the way," he said with a little uppity sniff, "I also got some unexpected praise about my new customers from the big boss."

When Jan and Stella were greeted at Donna's door two nights later, Donna was bubbly, and, in fact, sugary. She was wearing a gold satin blouse (with the top buttons undone) and leather pants.

Her white-blond hair hung in swirls to her waist. "Darlings," she said, hugging them both. "At last, we've gotten together. You've been bad, Stella girl! You just gotta get around more! Let's have a drink! What'll you have, doll? And I've got some little goodies for y'all." When Stella braved a glance at Jan, Jan rolled her eyes. The three of them laughed, drank, ate cheeses and paté, and got the brochures put together. At one point, Stella excused herself to go to the ladies' room because she wanted to pass an attractive desk to get a closer look at the pale green stationery that was placed there. When they were leaving, Donna told Stella that she just had to come back real, real soon and bring along her husband. She said she'd "just love to get to know him better."

When Stella got home, she ran to Jamie, threw her arms around his neck, and shrieked, "I'm so doggone lucky, I can't believe it!"

Jamie pretended shock. "Stella! Have you been drinking? If so, I like it! Have some more! I've been drinking, too, drowning my sorrows because you weren't here!"

They were so happy making love that night that Jamie just had to tell Stella, before they went to sleep, something he had planned to surprise her with a few weeks down the line. He just couldn't manage the secrecy any longer. "Remember Mildred Leverich?" he said. "She's the realtor who told me when this place here was available for lease. Your mother was sworn to secrecy because I left Washington early this week, took Wednesday off, and stayed with her so that I could get into the city to meet with Mildred for lunch and take a look at something without you knowing about it. She wanted me to see another place, and to buy it this time. She found us a very small but very nifty co-op. It's a Christmas present from me to you. We can move in by January." Jamie was glowing with pride and adoration for Stella's wide-eyed look of delight.

For the next little while, the timeworn apartment seemed like a palace to Stella as a result of her lofty feelings of exhilaration. She was a princess, and she was living a fantasy with her prince. The new one-bedroom co-op would have a very large mortgage in the busy area of Murray Hill, but the hurdles would be faced by two determined people who had love that knew no bounds.

The tale of Donna Schechter was simply a sad one. As Stella and Jamie chatted during the next several days, Stella learned that Jamie had been wise to Donna all the time, but didn't know about the contacts Donna had made with her. He had been approached directly by Donna through a call one night, asking that he and his "lovely wife" come over for a drink when she had known that Stella was at a night class. She pretended surprise, but suggested that he leave Stella a note and wait for her there. Having dealt with Mildred Leverich herself, Donna had learned, by chance, that Mildred would be seeing her neighbor, Jamie, and the date they would be meeting. She followed up and had pursued him to José's on 43rd Street, getting rebuffed there as well. Stella found out from one of Jamie's colleagues, also by chance, that he, Jamie, and their boss all had left midtown by taxi to have a discussion with a legal counsel the day he went to Lower Manhattan.

Stella considered taking the note in the green envelope back to Donna's door to tell her that she might need it for someone else, but she tore it up instead.

TWO:
ROLE REVERSAL

Jennifer and John Fendi and their two children had been transferred to a thriving and technologically-ambitious neighborhood
near the City of Vancouver. They had lived in the area for only five
months and still had many things to learn about its geography,
businesses, and the general pursuits of the people. Billy was just
four years old, so his social life was yet to come. Impressionable
Janice, however, had surprised and pleased her parents with her
ability to make new friends. She already had a best friend named
Suzanne, a girl from her class. They were inseparable, as only
twelve-year-old kids can be.

Unfortunately, when Janice visited Suzanne's house, although it
was only ten minutes away, she had to pass through a growth of
pine trees; she was out of sight for a few minutes because of those
trees. She had been told to be careful, and not to tarry, until she was
in view of Suzanne's house. Janice made herself familiar with
every little twist and turn of the path through the trees, and she
would hurry as fast as she could without being conspicuous. She
knew that her mother watched her go as far as the trees, and she
always turned to wave before entering the woods, even if her mother couldn't be seen. Her mom and dad were always anxious, and,
sometimes, her dad would take the car and wait on the other side of
the trees. That was unacceptable to Janice. "I'm not a baby, Dad,"
she said. "I can take care of myself. I watch what I'm doing. Really,
I do."

"We know, sweetheart, but we love you so much, and there are
some awful people about," her mother said. "We know you're
pretty grown up, so try to believe in us. We won't keep you away
from your friends, but we just don't want you to take any chances.

Let us drive you whenever we can, just the same." It was a difficult situation that many parents have to deal with. They try to avoid frightening their children, but then must give them frightening things to comprehend and stay away from. So, Janice had to walk a fine line between being trusted and being watched and advised. Everybody simply had to fight the unease, of course. It was important that Janice spend time with her friends. It was a problem for Suzanne also, as she would have to follow the path when the visits were reversed.

The Thanksgiving weekend had arrived, and Janice's grandma and grandpa were expected, as well as her Aunt Margaret and Uncle Hugh. Jennifer had also invited the Scotts, their neighbors from down the street, for the turkey dinner, telling everybody that holiday times are hard on lonely people. The Scotts had relatives only in Australia. Janice was eager to see Suzanne before the festivities started, and, besides, the guests weren't expected until four-thirty. It was just past lunchtime. There was a school trip coming up, and both girls were excited, wondering which gals and guys would be going. There was a lot to talk about.

It was a fairly nice day, not too cold, but the sky was heavy and rain was predicted when Janice set out for Suzanne's house. Her mother made her take her yellow slicker with the hood. Janice waved as usual and proceeded into the woods. Two partridges shot up in front of her, making the familiar noise that frightens, more from surprise than anything else. Two cyclists passed by also. Near the other side of the pines, Janice slowed down, happy to see Suzanne's street through the space which was opening up. However, at that moment, at her right, she heard a twig break. She looked to the right and saw a man standing a short distance away. He turned his head and moved away slowly. She began a slow run, feeling uneasy, and reached open ground. When she looked back, she saw the man again, but he was going in the opposite direction and soon disappeared.

She found Suzanne ecstatic. Her parents had just bought her a new bicycle. It was red and shiny. Her parents had wanted to wait until Christmas, but Suzanne needed to get to school on time. She had been reported as being late too often, and she promised her parents that the bike was just what she needed to fix the problem, so they consented and made a bargain with her. The bike was to be her reward for her promise, and it would be put away for quite some time if she didn't get a better report from the school personnel. In the excitement of admiring the new bike, Janice forgot about the man in the woods. After both took turns riding the bike, Suzanne wiped off a few smudges on one of the shiny red fenders with the bottom of her T-shirt, then they chatted, giggled, and commented on school friends.

Time went fast. Only when Janice was ready to leave did she remember the man in the woods. She didn't say anything to Suzanne. She had promised to help her mother set the table and be prepared to greet the guests, so she left about three o'clock. Her mother would be too busy to meet her, she thought, and her dad would be doing last-minute errands, so she decided to brave out getting back through the woods. Besides, she didn't want to scare her parents. She would run through the woods and get home as quickly as possible. In less than ten minutes, she was at their front door. She hadn't seen anybody in the woods at all, and she was proud that she hadn't made a fuss.

The days passed, and after many more trips between her and Suzanne's home, she didn't see any lone man in the area. Janice believed that the man was not going to be there anymore, and she let down her guard. Then, a few days later, she saw him when she was heading home. It was just beginning to get dark. He was close to where he had been before. Again, he avoided looking at her and turned away. She ran home and told her mother about him, and her mother reacted with shock. Holding Janice firmly by the shoulders, Jennifer spoke with a sharp voice, her eyes wide. "Janice, you mean you saw this man before? This was the second time? You know better than that. Tell me about him now, and don't go near the woods again unless we're with you. Janice, I'm surprised, and I don't ever want you to be so careless again. Now, describe the man to me."

"He didn't come near me, Mom. He looked all right, but I was scared anyway because all the adults talk about things like that and all us kids are scared to do anything!" Janice was upset and confused. "Aren't most men nice?" she said. "I don't even know why I was scared of him myself. He didn't come after me or do anything, but I was scared just the same."

When John arrived only minutes later and learned of the situation, he was almost frantic. He reprimanded Janice so that she was in tears. "You've seen him twice? Don't ever let me hear of this again," he said. "You're not going near your friend's place till we get to the bottom of this. What was he doing there? How long ago was this?" Without taking the time to reason or find answers, John took off directly to the woods to confront the man.

Just as he got within the pine growth, he saw a middle-aged man near the path. The man appeared normal, but slow-moving, and John, getting close, and in unthinking anger, peered directly at him; then abruptly stopped. The man's face was streaked with tears. His eyes were red, his face distorted. John stared, moved backward a little, and found himself saying, "Can I help you, Sir?"

"Oh, no…. No, thank you. I'm just looking for somebody." He then put his hands over his face and sobbed. John was flabbergasted, and he spoke with his heart, pointing to his house, "Please, I live just back there. Can I do something for you?"

The man straightened up and gave John a half smile. "I'll be okay," he said. "I come here often, looking for my daughter. She was fourteen years old when she disappeared. It was three years ago, and her abductor was caught. He's doing life now for her murder and another. The other little girl was found but they never found Annie, just some clothes." He sighed deeply, straightened up, looked directly into John's face and spoke, his voice breaking, "Annie was my life."

John took the man's hand and firmly held it to introduce himself. "John Fendi's my name, Sir. Do you want to talk to somebody about this? Please, come to my place. Come for dinner. My wife always wants to meet new people." He tried to smile a little and gently placed his hand on the man's arm to urge him on.

"Oh, no. No, thank you," the man said. "I'm Fred Craine. I live on the street just beyond that white house over there. My wife's expecting me, and we have our son and family coming this weekend. It's great to have them, but holiday times hit me hard. I can't help thinking about Annie."

"Well, of course not. But come another time and meet my family. Maybe we can help somehow."

"You're kind. I think you have a little girl. A little dark-haired girl, isn't she?" To John's nod, he added, "I see her at times coming from your direction. I try to avoid her so I don't scare her, but, sometimes, I'm just there. Thanks for your understanding. Happy to meet you." He moved off, and then he smiled, his face brightening.

John stood and watched him go, pained inside by the man's suffering. The man turned back and waved. "Watch over that little girl, John," he said.

THREE:
HERO

The pond in the park was easy to see now that the leaves had fallen. It was wide and deep after the rain. A noisy storm had passed through during the night, the warming of late summer clashing with a new front of colder weather. Penny Coleridge, a pretty and poised pale blond, smartly dressed in black pants and a gray cashmere blazer, was ready to go to work. She had not slept well because of the downpours that had come sporadically through the night, the thunder building up and subsiding. She now watched from her window as the morning traffic began to build off to the right, at the stoplight between Main and Slater Streets. As she often did, Penny took the time to look at the changing woodlands at the back of her apartment. The changes of the seasons affected her a great deal. She was a warm-weather *aficionada*, as she called herself, and, even though fall was near and the days were cooling off, she had to admire the beautiful sky at the moment. The rain had cleared, but the wind still whipped the white clouds. The contrast between the clouds and the blue, blue sky was intense, and Penny wanted to appreciate it for the moment.

Her apartment was on the second floor of the Willowbank Apartment building on the west side of Chicago, and from her dinette window, she wasn't quite able to figure out what the object in the wet leaves that had gathered in a culvert below was. She thought for a moment that it had moved, but she couldn't make any sense of it. There was a black mound with a blue patch that didn't seem to belong there. She glanced at her watch then and decided that she had better get going. She'd figure out later what the illusion was.

After locking up, Penny stopped. The object she had seen in the leaves bothered her. She wanted to find out what it was, but she had a feeling of unease and didn't want to approach it directly. She turned, unlocked her apartment door, and walked to her bathroom window, which was heavily curtained; only a very small slit was giving her a view. Now, the object had changed; it looked like a human figure. Her heart began to pound, but she stared, puzzled. At that moment, the figure slowly rose up, covered with a heavy shroud of leaves. From a kneeling position, it then bounded, keeping low, and headed for a copse of evergreens that skirted the pond.

What on earth…? What should she do? The figure was not large. Perhaps, it's a schoolchild running away? A thief who had fallen into the culvert in haste? She couldn't even describe her bewilderment. It was certainly a very strange sight. It would be hard to explain. She called the office, leaving a message that she'd be a bit late, and then she called Barbara Rose, her downstairs neighbor. "Barbara, I'm coming down," she said, and then she hung up.

Barbara was standing at her open door when Penny arrived and dashed in. "I need to talk to somebody in the building," she said. Barbara looked surprised and concerned, ushering her to a sofa. She knew that Penny was always on the go and wouldn't miss her daily routine unless it was very important. "I saw something that I can't quite explain," Penny continued. "There was a person outside, on the ground, hidden by the leaves. He got up and ran into the woods." Barbara's reaction was as expected. Did she think Penny had lost it?

Penny sat down and told Barbara how it had begun, trying to describe the bizarre scene as well as she could, noting her off-hand viewing of the lovely sky, and the object in the culvert, which she couldn't figure out. "I know you think I'm nuts, but honestly, Barbara, I'm as puzzled as you are. That's what I saw—just minutes ago."

"Let's go," Barbara said. "I believe you." They went to the area in question. There was no way of knowing how the figure could have been there. There was a large buildup of saturated leaves and perhaps a depression, but the water from the heavy rain was trickling into it. Their shoes were sinking in the soft terrain.

"Good grief!" Penny said. "Whoever was there had to be half frozen," she said, wrapping her arms around herself. "I can't believe it!" She was pointing to the evergreens, tracing the path the figure took to the park area, when a shout came from their building.

It was Judy MacDonald, the tenant on the first floor near Barbara's apartment. "Barbara, Penny, wait a minute." She ran to them, flushed and stressed. "Are you looking for somebody? I saw somebody a little while ago," she said when she got to them. "I was in the laundry room, and somebody passed the window. He had on a black jacket with a hood. That's all I could see, but I think he saw me and headed toward the woods. I raced to my dining room, but by the time I got to the window, he was nowhere to be seen." When they nodded, she continued, "Thank goodness you saw him, too."

Penny described again what she had seen, and all three women hurried back to Barbara's place, wondering whether or not to call the police. Anybody, of course, had a right to be near the apartment, but the unusual appearance, and immediate disappearance, of a strange person was not typical.

"Let's figure this out," Barbara said. "What exactly was the time that you saw this man, Judy? And you, Penny, what exactly was the time you saw him run?"

Penny responded first. "I was on my way to work. It had to be about a quarter to nine. Before I became alarmed, I was afraid I'd be late for work, and I locked up, but then I came back because what I saw bothered me. I didn't know what I was looking for, frankly. It was weird."

Then, Judy spoke. "It had to be just about that time, or maybe a little earlier. I had just put in some laundry after Fred left. He leaves at about 8:30. I'd say quarter to also."

"Then he was trying to hide in that cold, cold pile of leaves. You said you think he saw you?" Barbara said.

"Yes. Yes, I do."

Penny added, "And I happened to see him just after that—in the culvert. Man alive! He couldn't have lasted long in that, and he must have been awfully determined to hide. In fact, maybe he saw me at the window, too, when he ducked into the leaves. Oh, my gosh, let's call the police. This is crazy."

A tall, lanky officer named Frank Colonna, arrived and listened to the women who apologized several times for being unable to make any sense of what they had seen. Frank did not brush them off in any way and tried to get every detail from each of them. They all walked to the place near the culvert, which was now just leaves drifting in a shallow stream. "I'll start a report on this, but I'm not sure even dogs could follow a trail as washed away as this one," Frank said. He thanked the women with sincerity. "Everybody should follow up things that look suspicious," he said. "That's what we're here for. Give me your phone numbers, and I want you to keep in touch with me as well." He handed Penny his card. "I'll let you know if we find anything, and don't hesitate to call at any time. I'll give one of you a call tomorrow to make sure you're all okay. Lock up tonight."

The women left telephone numbers with Frank and thanked him for his quick response. "I'd better get to work," Penny said. "They'll be wondering where I am. And how do I explain this dumb thing?" The women parted then and promised each other that they'd call if anything else looked weird.

The following day, Frank called Penny and told her that they had no clues regarding anybody missing or anybody running from the law. It was a matter of a reverse police case. Instead of looking for an escapee, they were looking for a crime.

Two weeks later, before eight o'clock in the morning, Frank called Penny and asked her if she could come to the police station. He only said that it was with regard to the unusual sighting of the seventeenth. Penny was confused. *Will this puzzle never end?* she thought.

When Penny walked into Frank's cubicle, she was facing Frank and another officer, both of them smiling. Sitting in the corner chair was a teenaged boy. Frank introduced his colleague, Burt McShane, and then the young man, Jeff Franken. "Jeff," Frank said. "Tell Miss Coleridge who you are."

Jeff responded immediately. "I'm the guy who was in the ditch," he said. "I was trying to hide, but not from the police. These guys have all the information about it. I was, like, being chased, and I thought you might be the person I was running from when I saw you at the upstairs window. Another lady saw me also. I didn't know what to do, so I took a header into the leaves."

"Oh, my God," Penny responded. "How could you stand the cold, even for a few minutes?"

"I was paralyzed with the cold, and that's why I ran into the woods. I had to take my chances in that last sprint to the woods. I stripped off most of my clothes and stayed wrapped up in leaves until Burt here cruised by over at Slater Street. My cell phone was wasted, that's for sure, but I watched the openings near Slater and Haymarket, praying that I wouldn't have to wait long for a cruiser to pick me up. I guess it was only ten minutes or so, but it seemed like years! I didn't think I'd ever stop shaking." He was smiling a wan smile.

Frank broke in. "Jeff, let me fill in a little bit. I do believe that Miss Coleridge is befuddled, and who can blame her? I have to apologize to you, Miss Coleridge. I had to lie to you a few weeks ago about the person you saw. We knew who it was, but had to take a few days to work on it a bit before telling you about Jeff here. This young man is a hero, Miss Coleridge. At the ripe young age of fifteen, he is our hero. He opened up a big case with drugs and an arsenal. Someone in the gang was tipped off that he was in your building; they even knew the apartment number. We had to work fast. They had sent a woman to get him, and we tipped off Jeff and told him to get out. He thought you might be that woman."

"Oh, my God!" Penny was trying to get the facts together, and they were coming too fast. "Are you safe now?" she asked Jeff.

"I sure hope so," Jeff responded. This time, he smiled broadly.

Frank interrupted to ask somebody in the office for coffee for all of them. Then Burt McShane gave more details about the gang's hideout and Jeff's contribution. "Would you believe it?" he said. "Jeff watched the narcotics group through a basement window near his home on Third Avenue in town. He had seen several people come and go in a building, an old building that was up for demolition. He knew they were up to no good, but didn't know why. He photographed them with his digital camera at night while lying on the ground in the bushes, and he got very clear photographs of trades, stacks of money, and even faces. It was the morning just before you saw him in the ditch when we made the raid and nabbed five people. We haven't totaled up the street value of the drugs yet. It's enormous, and they had AK-47s and handguns of every size and description; guns and drugs just go together. A woman in this scheme was booked later. She was nabbed at the airport, in a line, buying tickets to New York. We had a surveillance team watching Jeff after he spilled the beans, but the perpetrators were easy to catch because of the film. There are more dealers involved, but we're close on their heels. It's a matter of time. Jeff has broken the back of a large network. He found the kingpins for us."

"Oh, my God!" It seemed that the expression was the only words Penny could summon up. "How did they get after you?" she asked Jeff. "How did they know where you were?"

"Frank and company were monitoring their cell calls. According to Frank, they had tracked me, and they were gunning for me at my friend's place. There was another gal involved, not the one at the airport. The gang's gal friend headed back to her parked car when she saw her buddies being busted. She had been heading for their hideout when she saw what was happening. Her friends were still being put into the police cars when she saw me clearly as her car moved passed us. I had led them to the building, and I was standing on the street with Frank."

Frank broke in. "Jeff recognized her. She was trying to make a run for it, but she was followed to the airport. She called somebody from her car and told her, a gal who turned out to be her sister, to 'track down the kid' who accompanied the police."

Jeff spoke then, "I had seen the woman face to face one night. She had just left the place. I was going toward the side of the building with my camera, but I changed course and went straight. At that time, I think she figured I was just a dumb kid from the neighborhood. After the bust, I had left to visit a friend in your apartment to tell him a bit about this." He glanced at Frank then and added, "I was told to keep some of this quiet for a time, but it sort of broke open when Frank called me on my cell phone and told me to run. My friend was freaked out. Frank said they'd try to get to me in time, but wasn't sure they could. He'd pick me up later. That's how I got out of the woods. I saw Burt's police cruiser. Frank was happy that you led them to me. He didn't let on. If you ladies hadn't called the police, I would have had to hope for the best that I wasn't caught, or else freeze to death in the woods, waiting for dark. I knew the cops would be in the area, but they didn't know which direction I had taken. They were fabulous at finding me hiding in that wooded area. That was the direction you led them to."

Burt spoke up. "One of our guys waited just a few minutes at his friend's apartment. The gal who arrived just minutes later was pretending to be a Jehovah's Witness, even carrying brochures. We were fanning out to close in on your neighborhood and pick Jeff up before you even saw him. We had cars north, east, south, west, and then you called. By the way, we knew Jeff had to be on foot. He doesn't even have a driver's license yet; he's not old enough." Everybody beamed at Jeff.

"I'm working on it," Jeff said with a bit of a shy look.

Penny took a big sip of her coffee. "This is too much," she said. "I think it's sinking in, but I still have to put the parts together. I can't believe it. All I wanted to do was look at the clouds." Everybody smiled with amusement.

"Frank, thanks so much for letting me in on all this," she added. "I never could have explained that strange figure if I hadn't heard this. I'm so glad that I did something right, even though I didn't know I was doing it." She continued, turning to Jeff, "If you were my brother, I would be mighty proud of you. I wish I had known all this so that we could have saved you from that cold plunge! So, this woman has been caught. Is anybody else after you?"

Frank broke in again. "We're all proud of him, Penny, and we're also watching him, and his family, carefully. He hadn't even told his mother what he was doing with his fancy camera. We'll watch him for a while, but you can't imagine how these unexpected events have cleaned up a ring of druggies that had everybody fooled. We were out to get them, but we were going in a lot of different directions until Jeff came to us. We've pretty well broken up the whole mess of them. They're either getting rounded up now, or they're already incarcerated."

Looking directly at Penny, Jeff added with a jocular twist of his head, "Worried about me, Miss Penny? I had, like, thought of disguise—dying my hair and growing a beard. I've always wanted blonde hair like yours." He stroked back his thick black hair with a sly look.

Everybody nodded enthusiastically when Burt McShane said, "If all our kids were like you, Jeff, we'd be out of business. We're going to make sure that you and your family are safe until all this is past history. Who knows? You might be able to join the force some day."

They told Penny that almost everything would be revealed in the evening papers. When everybody stood up to end the conversation, there was a feeling of camaraderie that was tangible. They had all undeniably contributed to a situation that was beneficial to all; the parts all fit together like a puzzle. A very dangerous crime complex had been crushed by everybody doing the right things without planning for them. There were warm handshakes all around. Everybody thanked Penny for calling the police. She gave Jeff a big hug and said, "Honey, next time you're in my neighborhood, don't take a cold swim. Come and say hello."

Driving home, Penny had to shake her head when she thought, *If things were different from what we experience nowadays, that wonderful boy could have come directly to me—or to Barbara or to Judy—to escape, but there is no denying that we would have been afraid of him. We would not have been able to believe that he was a mature young man in trouble, and we would have rejected him.* She repeated out loud with only herself to hear, "I just can't believe it. I just can't believe it."

She couldn't wait to talk to Barbara and Judy.

FOUR:
THE SCUTTLING OF DAD'S BOAT

Everybody surely agrees that personality traits are passed down from generation to generation. I think of my father with great pleasure, but I smile ruefully when I think of his indescribable impatience. Although he has passed on, I see him in myself, and, alas, I see him in my daughter. There's no skipping a generation here. I have only to go shopping in town to get road rage. If one thoughtless driver pulls out ahead of me, everybody is against me. I often have to apologize to those who do not know me well for my sharp remarks. Fortunately, those who do know me well can give as good as they get. As expected, if my daughter has so much as a bad hair day, she simply cannot forgive herself, and the world is caving in on her.

If matters didn't go as he had hoped, Dad would pace the floor with large strides and raise his voice several decibels. My mother would keep her composure, calmly suggesting that he was "flying off the handle" again. He was not particularly angry, except, perhaps, with himself. He was simply suffering from deep-set impatience. I recall a moment when some wire closet hangers became tangled up, as they often do. In a quiet rage that time, he twisted them all together and made a very large Chinese puzzle out of them. This was typical of the extent to which his impatience would reveal itself. All things considered, nothing serious came of his impatient moods; the consequences were seldom more dire than demolished wire hangers.

Dad was easily forgiven for this quirk of personality. My admiration for, and pride in, him was, and always will be, tremendous. When I look back, I see countless joys created by him. His inventive mind knew no bounds, and I have often wondered if there is a corollary wherein impatience naturally follows creativity. Probably, the inventive mind has so many facets trying to get out that impatience is inevitable.

To most people, Dad was known as a "pussycat." He was infinitely kind and was gifted with an unusually clever sense of humor. He could gather an audience, young and old, without any effort when his humor showed up. Childish jokes were acceptable, but nothing raunchy (it was a given in our home that foul language was simply not accepted). Two jokes, inane and moan-inducing, come to mind.

"Did you hear the story of the two holes in the ground?" After the expected, "No, what?" the answer was: "Well, Well!" And in the same vein, "Did you hear the story of the two men?" The answer was: "Hee, Hee!" My siblings and I loved his often repeated "He sat in the attic with his feet in the cellar—Longfeller." Such whimsy was infectious, and I can readily conjure up events of the past in which he was surrounded by children who found clean nonsense lots of fun.

We were a family of eight siblings. Dad was a tradesman, but was a master of most of the trades; we were never hungry or cold. What he could not buy for us, he invented. We were the envy of the neighborhood children in summer, when our backyard was bustling with family and friends. There was a teeter-totter and a huge swing (not hanging from a tree, but from a well-built structure). Then, we had the "hut," a small rough-hewn house about eight feet square, with a peaked roof, one door, and one window. Even a child-sized table was inside. The chairs were wooden boxes. Most wonderful was the swimming pool, probably the first in the county and built by hand. Four upright posts held an oversized tarpaulin, which was treated on the underside with a moisture-proof sealant. A garden hose filled it nicely. In winter, a large part of our backyard was a skating rink, snow banked around the edges so that, again, the garden hose was utilized. The rink, flooded each night, looked like glass.

One of Dad's creations still presents me with a little bit of shame and sadness. When I was about six years old, all the little girls on the street had doll buggies, some wicker and some elaborate with satin linings. I was desperate to have one, but the purchase of one was out of the question. Still.... Yes, Dad made me one. It was made with plywood, painted white, shaped with a little hood that moved up and down, and with wheels from an old wagon. Two small round windows on each side were made of celluloid. When I went outdoors with my favorite doll inside, I felt a little trepidation. What I suspected to happen did, indeed, happen. The children crowded around and began to point at the buggy, laughing, humiliating me completely. I hurried back home in tears as my father watched from the window. When I saw my buggy again, it was at the side of our coal bin, broken apart and waiting to be used as kindling. The whole experience was, of course, the "youth" thing. If I had my buggy now, I would encase it in glass for display.

As an adult, I also recall feelings similar to my now-realized, self-imposed regret over the buggy, imposed by an adult neighbor whose unthinking ignorance devastated me again when I was a child. It was a result of another of Dad's exceptional talents—the building of kites, the types that flew to the heavens. He specialized in large box kites, which were truly master works. In the far reaches, they were as steady as steel and small hands could not hold the strings without adult help. Dad even taught us how to send "messages" to the box kite, dwindled by space to a small pattern in the distance. Round pieces of paper, split and securely wrapped around the string, would be forced upward by the wind, and we watched as they were lost from sight, to be retrieved when the big kite was pulled in. I can only imagine what I would say today were I to go back to that day in which I was badly hurt. As I sat on a girlfriend's front porch on a hot summer day, one of the mothers remarked, "There goes that Mr. Burton again with his stupid kite." But could other children be blessed with such a father? It probably would not have registered with that woman if she had known that some engineers from the large hydroelectric power plant nearby had learned about and come to look over my Dad's kites.

Ironically, to this day, my family and I treasure events that were a direct result of Dad's impatience. There was even a cycle boat drama. We had grown up a little, and the most exciting invention yet was about to be launched. Dad had fashioned an old bicycle with wheels removed and replaced with pontoons on each side. Pedals were replaced by some sort of paddle system, and the structure became a strange but interesting catamaran sort of thing. I was mechanically challenged; I had no idea how it was all put together, and, even if I had, I would not be able to explain it. Strapped to the roof of the car, it looked like a weird two-wheeler. As usual, the neighborhood children followed us to the nearby creek, excitement mounting. Some were on bicycles, some driving with their parents.

My brother was the test boatman. He pedaled swiftly in the shallow edges of the creek, Dad close by in rubber boots up to his hips. The thing moved quite well until it was given a little nudge to deeper water, at which time the pontoons dipped too low. They had to be examined and repaired. After three or four trips back home for resoldering, etc., it appeared that the project was too unsafe for "water-biking," and my Dad had to admit failure. So deep was his self-defeat that he decided on the spot to put an end to his creation in the most expressive way he could manage. He decided to sink the cycle boat (in those days, there was not much to account for in dumping). He got a hammer out of his toolbox and a large nail. As he punctured one pontoon, his creation tipped slowly. Several more blows and both pontoons were under water. A push to deeper water did the trick. We all watched as our cycle boat slowly disappeared.

We all piled into the car and headed home, nobody saying a word. There would be other projects, and we knew that some of them would work. Dad's failures were few.

FIVE:
URSA MAJOR

"Man, oh man! Isn't this great, getting away from the routine for a bit? I can't wait to try out my new Remington. Not new, I guess, but wow, what a bargain!"

Stan Ballenger was a big man. Good-looking, with a neat dark jacket, his eyes showed attractive lines as he smiled. His companion in the passenger seat of the All-terrain Vehicle (ATV) was not so hefty, but was well built and a little untidy, with a toothpick dangling from his mouth. He wore the inevitable hunting man's plaid shirt.

Stan continued, "Marcelle had to lose out, by God. She wanted to visit her folks in Harrisburg this weekend, but hunting season doesn't happen all the time. She's gotta get used to it. As you know, she wants her own wheels, but I can't cough up insurance for two of 'em, especially with this baby I got here."

"Yeah," his companion agreed. "Hell, they want it all, don't they?"

Stan Ballenger and Bill Fielding had been friends for six years, taking their vacations on the deer-hunting trails. They were not good shots, but always returned home with something to show for their efforts. They brushed off any thought of maimed does. "Let 'em go!" Their trophies had to have racks. They followed the stags through streams, poison ivy, mud, and anything else that came up to get their quarry. After one hunting trip, they proudly took home a stag which had five bullet holes, two in the legs. "It's all in the game, Billy Boy, isn't it?" Stan said at one point, when they had abandoned a yearling that had fallen with a shot to the underbelly. It had leaped up and fled into heavy brush, pitching awkwardly.

Driving on in a misty rain, they continued their talk about

women in general, smiling patronizingly.

"Wanda is a good kid, just the same," Bill continued. "If she wants the van for the day, I usually let her drive me to work and keep it, as long as she's there to pick me up at five. I don't much leave her with a lot of bucks, however, when she takes the van. All they ever like to do is shop, these gals."

"I guess you're right," Stan added. "Even with the groceries, it took me a long time to get Marcelle to cut out the coupons. Damn it! They save a bunch of dough. She'd buy sirloin steaks for every meal if I let her. My mother used to buy ground beef by the ton, and she sure as hell didn't have to gussy up her meals for us. You know, we gotta teach the wives like they're kids again."

"Yeah, they learn eventually. They know men are smarter in everything except having babies," Bill replied. They interrupted that little discourse with a good chuckle until Bill followed up. "They've even showed pictures in the science news about men's brains being bigger. They can't fight the facts, right?"

The traffic was light for long stretches, and their spirits were high as they picked up speed. Stan said, with a joyful lilt in his voice, "We have only thirty miles now. We've done okay. I'm already tasting our dinner out of doors. What do you suppose we'll bag tomorrow? Wha'd'ya say we try for the biggest pointer yet?"

"You betcha," Bill said. "That's another thing about women, to get back on the subject. After we've driven through the High Road with the deer drapery tied all over our vee-hicle, I don't make a big fuss when Wanda doesn't want to deal with it. She usually doesn't even want to look at them. Her great-grandma would have pitched right in. Now, it seems that we all have to pay Joe Radner to dress 'em."

"Yes, I guess we all do that," Stan replied. "The gals today don't know how good they have it."

The men arrived at a spot that was familiar to them and pitched their tent, a case of beer close at hand. The air had the typical autumn chill, but the spitting rain was waning as they unpacked their gear. A radio blared country music, and each time they spoke, they had to shout above it. *What's to worry about in the wilderness?*

they had thought. They had driven 215 miles, and darkness had begun to close in on them. Nonetheless, everything went smoothly with the camp setup, and they were ready to quaff the beer and get the fire going. The fire, too, seemed to cooperate; it crackled underneath the tarpaulin they had stretched from the tent to their ATV, and it flickered with a savory scent . They hauled out two folding canvas chairs and sat back, their eyes drawn, as most are, to the rollicking flames.

"Boy, ain't this great?" Stan asked, taking off his National Rifle Association-emblazoned cap to brush back his hair. He replaced the cap more comfortably. "Marcelle's sandwiches can wait till tomorrow, don't you think? I sort of feel like some beefburgers after that drive. Need the protein for my biceps." He laughed, showing his arm muscles. Bill grinned in agreement. A tin pan, fifteen inches in diameter, held the four large patties. The rain had left the terrain wet, but that did not dampen their spirits. After eating grapes and homemade apple pie for dessert, they cleaned up and spread the plastic ground sheets, air mattresses, and heavy-duty sleeping bags into place; they had hung bright kerosene lanterns from the upper metal rods of the tent.

"I've gotta get out more. My shot's better than it was five years ago, but I need practice," Bill said. "You saw that beaut' I missed last year, remember? He was a ten-pointer if I ever saw one. What a big bastard he was!"

They moved outside again and sat quietly for a while, often gazing upward. The sky had cleared. They felt tired, but not eager to leave the sounds of the night. Because the woodlands were wet, they didn't douse the fire, enjoying the sputtering as it weakened. Before turning in, they saw the stars flickering.

Bill mused on the celestial scene. "I see the Big Dipper," he said. "It's just about all I know about astronomy. It's supposed to show the way to the North Star, but I wouldn't know which way."

They reluctantly closed up the tent. The "great stuff" would begin tomorrow. They fell asleep only after chatting a bit about their drive and *the* location, a spot that had been a winning deal for all hunters who knew its location. Bill also mentioned that they were glad that the gun lobby had held sway in several states. There had been announcements that all citizens had been given the right to carry concealed weapons at any place they chose. Sales had shot up. "Yep," Stan said. "The bleedin' hearts lost out, and the dames yakked about schools and libraries where children learned and played. Keep the kids home, I say, if you wanna make them scared of guns. Some men they'll be." And, as they often had before, they chuckled about the soaring purchases of firearms since the new administration had taken over, even before any serious compromise had threatened the gun lobbies.

It was Marcelle Ballenger who voiced alarm two days later. She had awaited a cell phone call the morning after the men were expected at the camp, and it had not come. That, in itself, was puzzling, but the recording also had come on with each call to Stan. Wanda Fielding also felt uneasy about the delay, although Bill didn't often check in right away. Would they leave their cell phones in the camp when they trekked through the bush? They didn't think so. The neighborhood rallied, and four men and the two wives headed for the campground in two cars, keeping a fast and steady pace, calling along the way in case they might pick up a connection.

They found the campground torn apart. The men held the women back forcibly when they saw the remains. They had a gory disaster to deal with; the more knowledgeable men agreed that, according to the paw prints, it had been a grizzly. The screaming women were driven back home by a neighbor, to await news of what had happened and to pull themselves together. A telling sign was found. There was a wild, blotchy note from Stan who had obviously struggled to write with charcoal on his groundsheet: "BIL DeaD...ShE got...I CANT......." It had been a she-bear. No gun had been fired. They never did find the sow.

SIX:
THE ACCIDENTAL INTERLOPER

Two strong arms lunged at Eva's shoulder, and two hands grabbed her jacket. She was dragged on her side along the roadside, which had been soaked by an afternoon shower. In just a matter of a few seconds, she was looking up from the grimy curb at two people; a young woman was helping her to her feet. The screech of a fast-moving car drowned out a voice. For the second time, the voice asked, "Are you alright?" Eva couldn't respond. She was stunned, and she stared at the crowd that was gathering.

"What happened?" she asked.

The young man spoke, his face showing fright. "You were almost run down, Miss. That car was heading for you. We had to grab you."

The young lady accompanying him wrapped her arm around Eva's waist as Eva staggered, unsteady. "You're all shook up," the young lady said. "So am I. That was just too close. C'mon, hon, get your bearings. Come and sit somewhere."

An older gentleman moved up at that moment and handed Eva a note, speaking to all three of them. "Take this," he said. "I got the last three letters of a license number, a Quebec plate. I couldn't catch the rest, but it looked like a word, a complete word. It ended in RNE. It was a Lexus. That driver knew what she was doing. It had to be intentional. Would you know a reason for this?"

It was only then that Eva became aware of the scene and found her heart pounding. She had seen only a flash of a black car, and it hadn't even registered with her when she found herself being pulled roughly to the ground. She was unaware of trying to brush a muddy patch from her sleeve as she stared in disbelief at the man who had spoken. She finally answered him. "A reason? No. Why....

what....? Do you really think someone tried to hit me?"

"Yes, I do." the gentleman said. "The car was parked right there at the curb, and the motor was idling. I thought it was strange. She took off from a dead stop. I saw the whole thing." He turned to the young lady who had helped her up. "I think you should take her for a checkup if you can. She took a terrible tumble. Thank God you were there. That was mighty fast thinking. You probably saved her life." He moved on, looking back in concern.

Eva didn't protest as the young couple guided her into an office building lobby, where they all sat on a long bench. The young man said, "I think he's right. We'll get a cab and take you to the hospital. We banged you up."

His companion then said, "Thank God we did, and thank God we saw what was happening. I still don't know when my instinct kicked in." Everybody laughed, finally.

Eva was treated at the Royal Victoria for her many contusions. Her new Lauren pants were torn and a bit bloodied by a scrape on her leg, but she was fine otherwise, and the hospital personnel praised her for her cool cooperation.

The young couple had introduced themselves as Fred and Greta Litroff, owners of a new, hopeful, start-up uniform supply company. Eva's office was not far away from theirs, and she explained that she was with a new firm also, in personnel. Fred and Greta stayed with Eva and waited for her examination to be finished. They chatted a bit and exchanged telephone numbers. "God bless you two," Eva said. "This is above and beyond—what you have done for me. I can't yet fathom what all this means, but if you hadn't been there, I don't know what would have happened."

"Follow up on this, Eva," Fred told her. "This is serious business, and I agree with that gentleman. I noted that he said 'she.' I vaguely remember a woman in the car. We're baffled, too, but watch what you're doing. That man was pretty sharp, wasn't he? I wonder who he was."

"I think I know who he was," Eva replied. "Those letters are on the back of a business card... uh, let me see.... GEORGE F. HALLOWELL & SON, INSURANCE BROKERS. And this is probably his address."

———

"Keep that business card and get busy with this, Eva," Greta said. Eva had insisted on their leaving her, promising that her fiancé would come for her. She hugged Fred and Greta with deep feelings before they parted. She then grabbed her cell phone from her handbag that Greta had carried for her along the way and called Josh.

Josh listened intently as she told him of the events. Without a pause, he said, "I'll be there as soon as I can. Stay with the crowds, sweetheart. Don't leave the hospital until I get there." He clicked off. Eva sat on a deep sofa near the entry, suddenly feeling very tired. Something was spinning in her head, and she began to unscramble it, her thoughts going back to Saturday night.

The previous Saturday, Eva Brigitte and Josh Zeller were in great spirits, planning to *finally celebrate* their engagement. They began a drive in a glorious sunset. They sang a little and listened to the radio, held hands, and beamed at each other every little while. They had a beat-up old Cadillac that still had a lot of miles to go, and they drove until they ended up almost eighty kilometers away from home. Josh knew of a beautiful dining place that they really couldn't afford, but he was planning to surprise Eva. He had said nothing before they pulled into a long, winding drive with elegant trees; it was a great arbor. He showed just a little bit of an upturn on the sides of his mouth. A big Georgian mansion with a very small sign appeared and became a revelation. *Le Jardin de Boudreau.* Eva was ecstatic.

Huge palms were embracing an atrium, and camellias were hanging low, their waxy leaves clinging to a filigreed iron screen, their blossoms a delicate pink. Small white lights sparkled everywhere on the dark oak passageway to the enormous dining room.

Their table was ready, but they requested the time to have a drink at the magnificent bar. Eva playfully said that under these circumstances, she wanted "a special, super-duper, extra-fabulous, bone-dry martini." Then, to Josh's surprise, she sat upright and stared. Moving toward the entrance was a face she knew. When their eyes met, Eva saw the man's jaw drop. A very sexy woman with long, black hair was clinging to his arm. The man turned quickly, ushered the woman into the vestibule, and they soon disappeared. It had been Greg Benedict, the head of Marvel Enterprises, one of her company's subsidiaries. She knew that he was in the throes of a bitter divorce, vociferously claiming infidelity on the part of his very wealthy wife. The woman with him was not his wife. Eva had to explain these facts to Josh because the event had been so visibly startling. "I wish I hadn't seen them," she had said.

Trying to make sense of these thoughts in the busy hospital lobby, Eva longed for Josh's presence. His office was on the other side of town. Her thoughts were whirling as her eyes locked onto a female figure that had a strange effect on her. The woman was outside, on the opposite side of the street, strolling, and glancing now and then at the revolving doors of the hospital. She was wearing wraparound sunglasses in the fading light. Eva knew no one of that stature or carriage, but something struck a chord, an ominous chord. Getting noticeably stiff from her fall, she had difficulty getting up and walking on a sore leg, but she stood, moved back, and kept the woman in view. Nearing the corner, the woman hastened her step and began to cross the street at the intersection. Eva was puzzled by her own reaction, but her intuition told her to get out of sight. The woman was heading for the revolving door. Eva hurried to a different doorway behind a large sign requesting contributions to a drive for the hospital's new addition. Staying behind a group of people, she dashed out the door. She bolted into a shop a little way down the block. It was a fabric store, and Eva walked quickly to the back of the store, smiling at a saleswoman and pointing. "I want to look at the drapery materials," she said. She examined the fabrics, keeping low and watching the front window. The woman did, indeed, pass the window, walking very slowly. It was too coincidental, and the woman looked entirely too blasé. Eva felt a little panic at that moment, wondering what she could do. She took note of the fact that the woman's hair was very dark, and there was a cloche placed above a chignon at the back. *Am I imagining things*, she thought, *or does she look like Greg Benedict's escort?*

Eva found an employees' ladies' room in a corner of the shop and slipped inside. There was a large frosted glass window placed rather high. She locked the door and decided that she was going to get out through that window. She suspected that she wouldn't have much time, so she quickly dragged a very large rubbish bin to the wall, turned it upside down and climbed atop, steadying herself on a hand drier. Her reach just made it to the lock, which she immediately turned. It was not a problem, but the window was stiff. She pushed the wooden frame with all her strength, feeling the pain of her wounds; she tried again, pounding the frame on both sides, cringing at the noise. Suddenly it gave, and it went right to the top. Eva was out in a nanosecond and landed on hard concrete in a narrow, dark alley.

She briefly stood still, terrified but alert as a deer, figuring out what to do. She was very quiet as she groped her way through garbage cans toward a bare light shining on a corner wall, and an opening facing Rue MacKay. Rats squealed, but she didn't give them a thought. She moved into a very dark spot near the street and called Josh. He picked up immediately. He was well on his way. "Josh," she said, almost whispering. "Listen, listen closely. Zero in on Maisonneuve and make a right at Rue MacKay. Find your way to an alley close to René Levesque. I'll be in that alley facing Rue MacKay. I'm going to watch for you from there. Got it? Rue MacKay. I'm not going to move from here until I see your car. Hurry." She cut the call and was silent. It was probably after fifteen minutes—an age to Eva—when Josh's Cadillac cruised near the entrance to the alley, and Eva made a dash for it. They took off before the door slammed.

Traffic was heavy in midtown. It took them twenty-five minutes to reach their second-floor walkup, Eva explaining her bizarre experiences all the way, keeping her head down. Josh said, "Are you thinking what I'm thinking?"

Immediately, Eva replied, "Yes. Saturday night."

Josh checked the dead bolt locks and the windows. He told Eva to keep her cell phone close, even near the regular telephone, which he told her not to answer if it rang. He needed to be at a meeting to sign a directive for his company just half a mile away. He would stop at the police precinct on the way home and would be back in about forty-five minutes, hopefully with a police officer. They'd explain their bizarre experiences to the police, and then they'd have a slow dinner at home. Eva finally felt secure. Being with her loving Josh had made her almost relax. *Even a cat burglar couldn't get into this place*, she thought. She hopped into a hot shower, and then wrapped herself up in a soft robe before she mixed a double vodka with lime juice. She put on a CD, a quiet jazz, and sat in a big chair, rehashing the amazing day—just a matter of hours—that had come upon her and Josh.

Eva was dozing a little when she sensed that something was wrong. She turned down the music a little. There was a faint sound near the back stairway that led to the laundry room and dumpster in the basement area. It was not the usual sound of couples sorting laundry or somebody playing music. She got up, glanced at the closed-circuit monitor above the door, and saw a woman slowly treading up the circular stairs; she was close. This, Eva now knew this time for certain, was the black-haired friend of Greg Benedict. The cloche was gone, but the black chignon was still in place.

Eva froze, but only momentarily. She had to have a weapon, even though the lock was secured on the door. She rushed, barefooted, without a sound, her head darting in every direction to find something strong. *Oh, for a baseball bat right now!* she thought. Under her potted dracaena plant, she spotted a twelve-inch tile, a leftover from a foyer job done months earlier. She carefully tilted the plant, pulled the tile out from under, and raced soundlessly back to the door with it. When she got there, an instrument was probing the lock, stopping sporadically, probably to listen. Eva made no sound, whatsoever, as she watched metal claws ease back the lock; she was praying that the beating of her heart could not be heard. The lock began to give. Eva's two hands held the tile high above her head. When the woman's black hair came into view, Eva brought the tile down with full force on the side of her head, heedless of a miserably-sore arm. The woman sprawled across the floor, a shiny gray gun sliding across the room and settling near the TV stand.

Eva stared in semishock as the woman lay still, her black hair loosened around her collar. Eva ran to the gun. She was frightened of even touching it, but she picked it up and held it as far away as she could get it, aiming toward the unmoving woman on the floor. She began to shake then, and she ran—fled, actually—out the door and down the stairs. She had to escape. She ran outside, gun in hand. A car pulling up to the curb had an amber light flashing. Directly in front was Josh who parked poorly and ran to her. Eva screamed, "Take it! Take it," and handed the gun to Josh who couldn't hide his total confusion. Why was she there, barefooted, and where did she get the gun? She was sobbing now, out of control, pointing upward toward their window.

He held her tight, handing the gun to the officer who had come from the police car. "Get hold of yourself, baby. Calm down. You're okay."

"She's upstairs. I think I killed her," Eva cried. The men looked at each other for what had to be less than a second, and then the policeman took the stairs two at a time to the open door on the second floor. Josh held Eva to him, tighter than ever before.

Eva had not killed Elise Gericault, but she had come close. Elise had not gained consciousness until she was being treated at the hospital. There was a massive concussion that would take a long time to heal, but she would have lots of time for healing while locked up. She would be charged with stalking and breaking and entering, in addition to two counts of attempted murder. Everybody knew that her accomplice would be out of circulation for a long time as well when the news came out during the next few weeks. While Elise was planning to take care of Eva, and her boyfriend if need be, Greg Benedict had been in the process of trying to dispose of his wife. They had both bungled very badly. Mrs. Benedict had learned of the plot and was waiting with armed officers when her husband entered the foyer of her home.

The two perpetrators had been too eager, desperately unschooled, and their plans had been too grandiose. Time had been of the essence. They were in possession of tickets to Paris for the following Friday to negotiate a villa in southern France. Enormous amounts of money had been transferred from the wealthy Mrs.

Benedict's accounts to a French bank before she had had the opportunity to settle her new power of attorney after redrawing her will and changing the beneficiaries. There would have been twenty-eight million dollars for Greg and Elise if they had succeeded in their plans.

Elise had gained access to the basement area of the apartment building by carrying a sack of laundry, waiting for somebody with a key, and telling a resident, Louise Ebert, who happened to pass by, that she was just moving in and didn't have a key for that entrance. In the police questioning, Louise remembered that the woman had dark hair, had parked her car too far from the curb, and was just going to "drop off" her laundry. Louise had also noticed that the license plate on the woman's car was distinctive: above *Je Me Souviens* was the word "NOCTURNE."

Without much more than their usual paychecks, Eva and Josh planned a huge party with all their friends, catered to the best that their budget could afford. Their guests of honor, Greta and Fred Litroff and Mr. and Mrs. George Hallowell, would be introduced.

SEVEN:
LITTLE RED RIDING HOOD

Joan figured that the latest ridiculous episode was the proverbial straw. Her husband was off with a group to California for a business meeting, and, after simmering for about three hours, Joan decided to pull it all together. She often got her head into focus just by sitting down in a quiet room and thinking, ignoring thoughts of things she should be doing. Her daughter was asleep now, and everything was quiet. She sat on the couch, put a cushion behind her head, and closed her eyes, drumming out a soft tattoo with her fingers on the end table. Her mind was made up, and she started to plan.

It had been Halloween night. Several children had come very early, before it was dark, their parents keeping close watch from the sidewalk. The shining eyes and excited voices enhanced the spooky scenes of jack-o'-lanterns and witches decorating the neighborhood porches. Fake wigs and bright makeup were simply essential, and the children were wonderful. Kim, at three and a half, had been fascinated with the costumed children, and she had asked her mom if she could try on Judy's mask. Judy was a neighbor, a little girl just Kim's age. Judy had offered her mask to Kim after asking why she couldn't go with them for trick or treating. Judy's mother had moved forward and gently urged her daughter not to interfere, but Joan just smiled. "Hi, Liz," she said.

When the children and parents had continued down the street, Joan said, "Kim, honey, we're going to get you a costume, and we'll catch up with your friends." She wrapped Kim's little blue windbreaker around her, and then put on her own jacket before she rifled through her handbag for some money. She found only a dollar and sixty cents. *Damn it*, she thought, *I have to find some money.* She looked in the cupboard where she often placed change for the newsboy. There was nothing there. She stood and thought hard, her hand raised to her chin. She ran into the bedroom and looked through another handbag where she found sixty-two cents more. "Damn it," she said aloud. "I'm going to call your dad." Jerry kept everything private and personal, downstairs, in his home office. He had credit and debit cards, but they were in his name only. Kim watched her mother's every move, her face eager and hopeful.

There was no reply in Jerry's room at the Radisson. With the three-hour difference in time, Joan guessed that he would be having a late lunch meeting with his colleagues. She dared not call him on his cell phone. She had left a message in his room, but felt desolate. *Why did I even mention it to Kim?* she thought. She stooped down and put her arms around her daughter, gently telling her they'd just have to stay home. "Mommy's sorry, honey. I'll get something nice. Want some of our chocolate?" Kim's eyes filled with tears. Even her shiny gold hair looked limp and sad. The doorbell rang again, and Joan was glad to be sidetracked. The telephone rang as she was opening the door. She smiled at a pirate and two princesses, one with a tiara, and said, "Help yourselves. Gotta answer my phone." Small hands dived into the candies on the table.

"Oh, Jerry, I'm so glad you called."

"What's up?" he said. "I picked up your message from a meeting."

"I need some money. Just a little bit. Would you know of any hanging around? Do you have a few dollars here anywhere? I promised Kim I'd take her out trick or treating, and she doesn't have any kind of costume."

"You've got to be kidding," Jerry responded. "She's three years old and you want to take her out on the street? Forget it. You called me for that?"

"Some of the little kids are out with their parents. They're loving it, and they want Kim to go."

"I think it's stupid," he said. "I left you enough to do you till I get back. I'll see you Sunday." He clicked off. Joan was burning with embarrassment and anger, annoyed with herself for having even called him. She should have known.

Kim was resigned now, but Joan felt like she was betraying her little girl. Her face was so innocent, and so forlorn. Joan went to her, took her hand, and said, "Let's go, my beloved. We're going to do something about this." She drove directly to the dime store, praying that she could find some cheap little piece of material to throw together as a witch's dress, or whatever. Luck was with her. In the ragged leftovers of costumes, she found a red plastic cape with a hood, halfway out of its package. "Kim, sweetheart, look at this," she said, "You can be Little Red Riding Hood!" The cape was too big, but it was only $1.99, and, even with the tax, Joan had enough. To her delight, the cheerful saleslady gave her the cape for a dollar, smiling knowingly as Joan counted out her change. "It's only the dregs left in the costumes now, honey," she said.

Driving home, Joan was proud that she had not let the opportunity pass. A little piece of plastic would give a little joy to her beloved girl. The roominess of the oversized cape was a boon over Kim's windbreaker, but the cape dragged on the floor, and they both laughed. "No problem, my love. I'll fix that in a jiffy," her mother said. She cut off six inches of the cheap plastic hemline. The hood kept falling back, so she tied a skinny scarf around it and made a headband. They didn't have a mask, but that didn't matter. Kim was a fine-looking Little Red Riding Hood. In hardly any time at all, she was walking with her mother, her hand holding a small plastic bag. Joan put a UNICEF pumpkin around her other tiny wrist. The plastic pumpkins had been given to all the children at the local hardware store.

Jerry had left Joan with forty dollars and a near-empty gas tank. There was ample food; with the never-ending frugality of Jerry, Joan had become an excellent manager. But this miserly scene for Kim's Halloween was just another degrading put-down in an endless stream of hurtful insults Joan suffered, such as being told that she was a "shopaholic," a "big-time spender," and a "waster of money" all over town. He hadn't even suggested excuses for the fifteen hundred dollars he had spent four months earlier on the two cars for his antique Lionel train set which "would just about make his collection complete." The old photographs gracing his office walls—trains and depots of the past—had also been costly, especially with the framing materials of the highest quality.

Harvey Schmidt, the affable lawyer who helped Jerry with his business and taxes, had met Joan one day and had asked her to have a cup of coffee with him. To Joan's surprise, he had opened up to her about Jerry, and told her that she should take her own life into account more aggressively.

"It's not my place to intrude," he said. "And I may be out of line professionally, but you should think of yourself more, my dear. You need to think of something that would be good for you for a change." He had a dark and serious look about him as he put a fatherly hand on hers. "There are three of you, not just one." This was an obvious put-down for Jerry, and Joan felt uncomfortable, but she understood. Harvey seemed to want to say more, but was reluctant. Joan smiled lamely and suspected that Jerry had told him about the fracas she had had with Jerry two weeks earlier, Jerry thinking that another man would believe it to be the "macho" thing to do. Jerry had slapped her across the mouth as he told her to knock it off about needing more house money. Joan had cowered for two days, afraid of him. He had apologized profusely, of course, but Joan seethed inside.

Joan's mother despised Jerry and had vehemently opposed their marriage. She still did her best to avoid her son-in-law. Joan knew that she expected, and indeed hoped, that the marriage would break up. Joan's father was noncommittal for the most part, but, one day, he had confided in his daughter that Jerry was a little "scary." Joan had laughed it off.

The following morning, the day after Halloween, Joan buckled Kim into the car seat. They drove past sad-faced pumpkins and flapping ghosts to Harvey Schmidt's office, and then to the service station where everybody knew her. Her spirits rose when she saw the big smiles on the men in the garage and heard their cheerful greetings. John, the manager of the shop, said, "No problem" when Joan asked that he put the charge for a fill-up on Jerry's account. She stopped at the liquor store on the way home and picked up several empty boxes.

After Kim fell asleep that night, Joan gathered more boxes from the basement, plus an old suitcase she had owned before she was married, and began to pack. She swept through the house as quietly as she could, picking up everything that was of value, and boxed and placed all of it in the car. The trunk and the back seat were loaded when she went to Jerry's office downstairs. She took all the train and depot pictures off the walls, piled them in the middle of the floor, and then dismantled as many train components as she could manage. She dragged them to the center of the room, piling them on top of the pictures. There was a crunch of picture glass.

When Kim woke up the next morning, Joan grabbed her and swung her around, and then she hugged her super-tight. Kim looked a little surprised, but she giggled. They had a big breakfast with scrambled eggs and crispy bacon, which Kim loved, and then Joan placed the dishes in the sink and left the pans on the stove. She picked up the car keys, looked around, took Kim by the hand, and then went into the garage where she buckled Kim into her car seat and backed the car out, stopping in the driveway. "I'll be back in a minute, sweetheart," she said to Kim. She handed a shabby teddy bear to Kim, tossed her handbag onto the floor of the car, and went back into the garage where she picked up a large gasoline can, went to Jerry's office, and spread the gasoline in all directions on top of his train parts and pictures. She then tossed a flaming, rolled-up paper on top, heard the "swoosh" of the fire, and fled to the car.

A few blocks down the street, Joan saw Jo-Anne Frye walking her dog. She rolled down the window and shouted to her, "Jo-Anne, sweetie, be a love and call the fire department; 262's on fire." She blew a kiss and drove on, smiling at Jo-Anne's open-mouthed reaction in the rear-view mirror.

Joan and Kim merged into the traffic on the highway and headed out.

SEPTET

MYRTLE M. BURTON

This book is a result of creating characters in random locations, devised to form an anthology. It is the author's desire that readers of all ages will enjoy getting lost for just a little while in brief episodes from somebody else's imagination. There are seven settings and seven adventures. One of the stories is non-illusory; the author's father was so colorful a character that she found it necessary to feature him in the only real-life story of the collection. You will be introduced to fictional new friends in the other mini-stories.

Myrtle M. Burton was born during the Great Depression, sixth in a family of eight siblings. Her parents were hard-working and exacting. Family pursuits through the years were attained by becoming creative in an environment of tenuous means, resulting in the love of all things inventive and aesthetic. Myrtle earned a Bachelor of Fine Arts degree by determination. She took out loans, studied and wrote while working full-time in office venues and taking care of a family.

Ms. Burton is a mother and a grandmother. She has dual citizenship from Canada and the United States.

Cover Design by Jennifer Tena
ISBN: 978-1-4349-9881-1 • $9.00 US / $11.00 CAN

ROSEDOG BOOKS
701 SMITHFIELD STREET • PITTSBURGH, PA 15222